W9-BDP-450

DATE DUE

the TREASURE ON Gold Street

EL TESORO EN LA CALLE ORO

A Neighborhood Story in English and Spanish

the TREASURE ON Gold Street

EL TESORO EN LA CALLE ORO

A Neighborhood Story in English and Spanish

By Lee Merrill Byrd

Illustrations by Antonio Castro L.

translated by Sharon Franco

CINCO PUNTOS PRESS
www.cincopuntos.com

"Make new friends but keep the old,
One is silver and the other's gold."

That's what Momma and Daddy always say when they tell people the name of our street. It's Gold Street in El Paso and our house is on the corner. Grandma and Grandpa live next door. That's where Momma grew up.

My name is Hannah. I have a baby brother. His name is Johnny. Sometimes in the afternoon Johnny cries so loud you can hear him all up and down Gold Street. If Momma can't get him to sleep, Grandma comes across her driveway to our house and picks him up. She puts his head against her shoulder.

Together we walk up to Silver Street where the big trees make it cooler. By the time we get there, Johnny is asleep.

Then we turn around and walk back home. Grandma puts Johnny in Momma's arms. Everything is quiet for a while.

—Los amigos que tienes son un tesoro
Los nuevos de plata, los viejos de oro.—

Así dicen mi mami y mi papi siempre que hablan con alguien del nombre de nuestra calle. Es la calle Oro en El Paso y nuestra casa está en la esquina. Mi abuelita y mi abuelito viven al lado. Es ahí donde mi mami se crió.

Me llamo Hannah. Tengo un hermanito. Se llama Johnny. A veces, por la tarde, Johnny hace tal escándalo llorando que lo oyen por toda la calle Oro. Entonces, si mami no puede calmarlo, mi abuelita viene a nuestra casa y lo levanta. Le recarga la cabeza en el hombro de ella.

Caminamos juntos hasta la calle Plata donde está más fresco bajo los grandes árboles. Ya para cuando llegamos, Johnny está dormido.

Entonces nos volvemos y regresamos caminando a la casa. Abuelita pone a Johnny en los brazos de mi mami. Todo se queda tranquilo por un rato.

Then Isabel comes over to play.

Isabel and her mother Mrs. Favela live next door to Grandma and Grandpa. Everybody calls Mrs. Favela Bennie.

Isabel and Bennie hold hands all day long. They hold hands when they walk up and down Gold Street. They hold hands when they sit on their front step, side by side. They hold hands when they pass by my house.

Bennie makes burritos with huevos and chorizo for breakfast every day. That's what Isabel tells me. Sometimes she tells me in English and sometimes she tells me in Spanish because she speaks both, just like me.

Luego Isabel viene a jugar.

Isabel y su madre, la señora Favela, viven al otro lado de mi abuelita y mi abuelito. Todos le dicen Bennie a la señora Favela.

Isabel y Bennie andan tomadas de la mano todo el día. Van de la mano mientras caminan de arriba para abajo por la calle Oro. Están de la mano cuando se sientan en el escalón al frente de su casa, una junto a la otra. Van de la mano cuando pasan por delante de mi casa.

Bennie prepara burritos con huevos y chorizo para el desayuno todos los días. Es lo que me dice Isabel. A veces me lo dice en inglés y a veces me lo dice en español, porque ella habla los dos, así como yo.

Bennie is very old.

Grandpa says that the older Bennie gets, the more she shrinks.

"One day," he says, "she'll shrink so much she'll blow away, especially in the spring when the winds blow so hard in El Paso."

I think that's why Isabel holds Bennie's hand—so Bennie won't blow away, especially in the spring.

Bennie es muy vieja.

Abuelito dice que mientras más viejecita, más chiquita se pone.

—Un día —dice— se achicará tanto que el viento se la va a llevar, sobre todo en la primavera cuando hay tanto viento en El Paso.

Pienso que es por eso que Isabel le toma la mano a Bennie—para que el viento no se la lleve, sobre todo en la primavera.

Isabel is old too, but not as old as Bennie. I love Isabel because she is big like a grown-up but she plays with me like a friend. Momma says that when she was growing up on Gold Street that was why she loved Isabel too.

Isabel hangs the wash in her backyard every morning after breakfast. Bennie sits on the front step while Isabel hangs the wash. Every few minutes Bennie calls out ISSAAABELLLLL. I can hear her at my house.

Grandma says that Isabel gets lost in the backyard when she's hanging the wash and that's why Bennie has to call her. I think that's why Bennie holds Isabel's hand all the time—so Isabel won't get lost.

Isabel también es vieja, pero no tanto como Bennie. Isabel me cae bien porque es grande como persona mayor, pero juega conmigo como amiga. Mami dice que cuando ella era pequeña y vivía en la calle Oro era por eso que a ella también le caía bien Isabel.

Isabel tiende la ropa en el patio de atrás cada mañana después del desayuno. Mientras tanto, Bennie se sienta en el escalón de en frente. A cada rato Bennie grita ISSAAABELLLLL. La escucho desde mi casa.

Abuelita dice que Isabel se pierde en el patio mientras tiende la ropa y por eso Bennie tiene que llamarla. Creo que es por eso que Bennie le toma la mano a Isabel todo el tiempo—para que no se pierda.

One Saturday morning, Bennie and Isabel passed by my house. I stood on my porch and called, "How about if I hold hands too?"

They said okay. Daddy said I could go walking with them. I held on to Isabel's hand and Isabel held on to Bennie's.

We walked from our corner of Gold Street all the way down to the next corner.

There was a big yellow ball that didn't belong to anyone on the other side of the street.

"Pelota," said Isabel. She let go of my hand.

"¡Cuidado!" said Bennie. "You'll get run over."

She wouldn't let go of Isabel's hand.

Un sábado por la mañana, Bennie e Isabel pasaron frente a mi casa. Yo estaba parada en el porche y les grité: —¿Qué tal si yo también voy con Uds. de la mano?

Dijeron que sí. Papi dijo que podía ir a caminar con ellas. Yo iba tomada de la mano de Isabel y ella de la mano de Bennie.

Caminamos de nuestra esquina de la calle Oro hasta la esquina de la próxima calle.

Había una gran pelota amarilla que no era de nadie al otro lado de la calle.

—Pelota —dijo Isabel. Me soltó la mano.

—¡Cuidado! —dijo Bennie—. Te van a atropellar.

No quiso soltar la mano de Isabel.

Bennie looked both ways, one way for her and the other for Isabel.

"Stay here," she told me.

Then she and Isabel crossed the street and got the yellow ball. Isabel held it in her arms. But then she had no hands for us to hold so I held on to her pocket and Bennie held on to her shirt.

We went back up Gold Street. Isabel saw a little teddy bear on the sidewalk.

"Oso," she said. It only had one leg. She picked it up. We put the bear in Bennie's pocket.

Bennie miró calle arriba y abajo, a un lado por ella y al otro por Isabel.

—¡Espérate aquí! —me dijo Bennie.

Las dos cruzaron la calle y recogieron la pelota amarilla. Isabel la llevaba en los brazos. Pero así no podíamos tomarla de las manos. Entonces agarré su bolsillo y Bennie agarró su camisa.

Caminamos de regreso por la calle Oro. Isabel vio un osito de peluche en la acera.

—Oso —dijo. Tenía una sola pata. Lo recogió. Metimos el osito en el bolsillo de Bennie.

We walked past Bennie and Isabel's house and then past Grandma and Grandpa's. Something was sitting in the flowers. Isabel stopped again.

"¿Qué es?"

I picked it up. It was a block. It used to be in my toybox.

"B," said Bennie. "Ball."

"Burrito," I said. "I'm hungry."

"Baño," said Bennie. "Hurry. I've got to go right now."

Isabel laughed so hard she almost dropped the yellow ball. We put the block in my pocket.

Caminamos por la casa de Bennie e Isabel y luego por la de mi abuelita y abuelito. Había algo entre las flores. Isabel se paró otra vez.

—¿Qué es?

Lo recogí. Era un bloque. Antes estaba en mi caja de juguetes.

—B —dijo Isabel—. Balón.

—Burrito —dije—. Tengo hambre.

—Baño —dijo Bennie—. Apúrense. Tengo que ir al baño.

Isabel se rio tanto que casi dejó caer la pelota amarilla. Metimos el bloque en mi bolsillo.

Then we came home. Bennie went to the bathroom. After that we sat on the front porch. Momma made some lemonade and then we looked at all the things that Isabel had found. Isabel liked the teddy bear the best.

Bennie said: "I tell her, 'Isabel, you're not a little girl. You're a big girl. You don't have to play with dolls anymore.'"

Then Bennie smiled so much her eyes shut and Isabel smiled a big smile and laughed real loud.

"Oh-oh," said Momma. "Isabel, you're laughing so hard, you're going to fall off the front porch."

So then Isabel and I went inside and got a book and sat down on the couch while I read the book. It was a funny story, all about people who went on a walk and found wonderful treasures.

Entonces llegamos a mi casa. Bennie fue al baño. Después nos sentamos en el porche. Mami hizo limonada y luego miramos todas las cosas que Isabel había encontrado. A Isabel el osito le gustaba más.

Bennie dijo: —Le digo, 'Isabel, ya no eres niñita. Eres grandota. Ya no tienes que jugar con muñecas.

Bennie sonrió tanto que se le cerraron los ojos, e Isabel sonrió también y se rio fuerte.

—¡Cuidado! —dijo mami—. Isabel, te estás riendo tanto que te vas a caer del porche.

Entonces Isabel y yo entramos y escogimos un libro y nos sentamos en el sofá mientras yo leía el libro. Era un cuento chistoso sobre algunas personas que fueron de paseo y en el camino encontraron tesoros maravillosos.

The next day Isabel and Bennie came over again. Isabel and I sat at the dining room table and colored. I drew a picture of Isabel and me and Bennie walking down Gold Street. Isabel drew a picture of a queen with a crown on her head.

"¿Quien es?" I asked her.

"Una reina," said Isabel. "Me!"

Then I asked Momma if we could get in the pool. She put it out on the front porch and filled it up with water. I took off my shorts and shirt.

"Take off your shirt and pants," I told Isabel. She shrugged her shoulders.

"Get in, Isabel!" I told her.

"She's too big," said Bennie, so Isabel sat next to me while I played in the pool.

Al día siguiente Isabel y Bennie vinieron de nuevo a la casa. Isabel y yo nos sentamos a la mesa del comedor y coloreamos. Hice un dibujo de Isabel, Bennie y yo caminando por la calle Oro. Isabel hizo un dibujo de una reina con corona en la cabeza.

—¿Quién es?— le pregunté.

—Una reina —dijo Isabel—. ¡Yo!

Entonces le pedí permiso a mi mami a jugar en la piscina. La colocó en el porche delantero y la llenó de agua. Me quité los pantalones cortos y la camisa.

—Quítate la camisa y los pantalones —le dije a Isabel. Se encogió de hombros.

—¡Métete, Isabel! —le dije.

—Es demasiado grande —dijo Bennie. Entonces Isabel se sentó junto a mí mientras yo jugaba en la piscina.

There's another girl on Gold Street I like a lot, too. Her name is Erica. She lives across the street. She is bigger than me. She has a scooter and she rides up and down in front of her house all day.

I always stand in front of Grandma and Grandpa's house, right on the curb, and call out, "Erica, can you come over and play?"

"No," she says. "My mother says I can't cross the street."

"When can I cross Gold Street so I can play with Erica?" I always ask Momma.

"When you get bigger," she says. "And anyway, you have Isabel. There aren't any friends better than Isabel."

Hay otra niña que vive en la calle Oro que me cae bien. Se llama Erica. Vive en la casa de en frente. Ella es más grande que yo. Tiene una patineta y patina de arriba para abajo frente a su casa todo el día.

Yo siempre me quedo parada delante de la casa de mi abuelita y mi abuelito, justo en el bordillo, y le grito:
—Erica, ¿puedes venir a mi casa a jugar?

—No —dice—. Mi mamá no me permite cruzar la calle.

—¿Cuándo puedo cruzar la calle Oro para jugar con Erica? —le pregunto siempre a mami.

—Cuando seas más grande —dice—. Y de todas formas, tienes a Isabel. No hay mejor amiga que ella.

But then one day Erica's mother asked my mother if I could come and play. Momma and Johnny walked me across the street.

I was so excited. I had never been to Erica's house before. She has lots of dolls.

She has lots of books, too. I lay down on her bed and started to read one out loud.

Erica said, "You can't read."

"Yes, I can," I told her.

"Well," said Erica, "that's not what that book says."

Then we went in the back yard to play Store. I was the lady who was selling pretty dresses and Erica was the beautiful girl who was going to buy one. I wanted to be the girl, but Erica said I wasn't old enough yet.

Pero un día la madre de Erica me invitó a jugar a su casa. Mami y Johnny me acompañaron a cruzar la calle.

Estaba muy contenta. Nunca había estado en la casa de Erica. Tiene muchas muñecas.

También tiene muchos libros. Me acosté en su cama y empecé a leer en voz alta.

Erica dijo: —No sabes leer.

—Pues, sí—le dije.

—Bueno —dijo Erica—, pero ese libro no dice eso.

Luego fuimos al patio de atrás para jugar a las tiendas. Yo era la mujer que vendía vestidos bonitos y Erica era la chica bonita que iba a comprar uno. Yo quería ser la chica pero Erica dijo que yo era muy chiquita todavía.

Then we went out front to play. Isabel came over. I ran to hold her hand.

"Isabel, are you lost?" I asked her. "Where's Bennie?"

Erica told Isabel that she would have to come back later because we were playing.

"Can't Isabel play?" I asked.

"No," said Erica. "She's too old."

Then she said to Isabel, "Isabel, how come you aren't married?" And she laughed.

Isabel shrugged her shoulders and laughed, too.

Then we heard Bennie calling. "ISABELLLLLL."

"Run, Isabel," Erica's mother said. "Your mother is calling you."

"I used to play with Isabel," said Erica after Isabel left, "but I don't anymore now that I am big."

Luego fuimos a jugar frente a la casa. Vino Isabel. Corrí a agarrarle la mano.

—Isabel, ¿estás perdida? —le pregunté—. ¿Dónde está Bennie?

Erica le dijo a Isabel que volviera más tarde porque estábamos jugando.

—¿No puede jugar Isabel?

—No —dijo Erica—. Es demasiado grande.

Entonces le dijo a Isabel: —Isabel, ¿por qué no te has casado? —Y se rio.

Isabel se encogió de hombros y se rio también.

Luego oímos a Bennie gritar: —¡ISABELLLLLL!

—Corre, Isabel —dijo la madre de Erica—. Tu madre te está llamando.

—Antes yo jugaba con Isabel —dijo Erica después de que salió Isabel —pero ahora que soy grande ya no.

The next Saturday was Isabel's birthday. Daddy said she came to our house and knocked on the door before the sun came up just to tell him. I was still asleep. Daddy said he was still asleep, too.

"Oh-oh," Momma said. "I forgot Isabel's birthday." As soon as the store opened, we went and bought her some presents. I picked out a doll with a pink dress. Momma bought her a book with big pictures. She bought her a cake with Happy Birthday written on it.

When Isabel and Bennie came walking up Gold Street, I gave Isabel the doll and Momma gave her the book.

El sábado siguiente era el cumpleaños de Isabel. Papi dijo que ella había venido a nuestra casa antes de que amaneciera sólo para decírselo. Yo estaba dormida todavía. Papi dijo que él también estaba dormido.

—¡Ay! —dijo mami—. Se me olvidó el cumpleaños de Isabel. —Tan pronto se abrió la tienda, fuimos y le compramos unos regalos. Escogí una muñeca con vestido rosado. Mami le compró un libro con grandes dibujos. Le compró un pastel que tenía escrito: Feliz Cumpleaños.

Cuando Isabel y Bennie vinieron caminando por la Calle Oro, le regalé la muñeca a Isabel y mami le regaló el libro.

"Mira," said Bennie.

We looked up. Erica was coming to our house. Her mother watched her cross the street. Erica was holding a present.

"Happy Birthday, Isabel," she said when she got to my house.

"How did you know it was Isabel's birthday?" I asked.

"She told me!" Erica said. "And she told me to come get some cake!"

"But how did you know you were having cake, Isabel?" I asked.

Isabel shrugged her shoulders and laughed.

—Mira —dijo Bennie.

Todos miramos. Erica venía a la casa. Su madre le miró cruzar la calle. Erica llevaba un regalo.

—Feliz cumpleaños, Isabel —dijo al llegar.

—¿Cómo sabías que era el cumpleaños de Isabel? —pregunté.

—¡Me lo dijo ella! —dijo Erica—. Y me invitó a venir a comer pastel.

—Pero, ¿cómo sabías que ibas a tener un pastel, Isabel? —le pregunté.

Isabel se encogió de hombros y se rio.

Then everybody came over: Daddy and Grandpa and Grandma and all the kids in the neighborhood.

"Are we in time for Isabel's birthday cake?" Grandma asked.

Momma brought out the cake with one really big candle in the middle. Daddy lit it.

"Here's to Isabel, the treasure on Gold Street," Momma said.

We all sang Happy Birthday and Isabel made a wish and blew out the candle.

"What did you wish for?" asked Bennie and she smiled so big her eyes disappeared.

"More presents!" Isabel said.

Entonces llegaron todos: Papi y Abuelita y Abuelito y todos los niños del vecindario.

—¿Llegamos a buena hora para el pastel de cumpleaños de Isabel? —preguntó mi abuelita.

Mami trajo el pastel con una vela grande metida en el centro. Papi la prendió.

—Para Isabel, el tesoro de la calle Oro —dijo mami.

Todos cantamos Feliz Cumpleaños e Isabel pidió un deseo y sopló la vela.

—¿Qué pediste? —preguntó Bennie y sonrió tanto que se le desaparecieron los ojos.

—¡Más regalos! —dijo Isabel.

happy Birth day Isabel

Then Momma brought out her scrapbook.

"Look, kids," Momma said. "Do you know how Isabel knew she was having a cake?" Momma pointed to a picture of Isabel blowing out a candle on a birthday cake.

We all crowded around Momma.

"See this picture?" she asked. "That's next door, at Grandma's house, where I grew up."

"And that's me!" I said, pointing to the girl who was sitting next to Isabel.

"No," said Momma. "That's me! I was just as old as you are right now, and Grandma bought Isabel a birthday cake, just like she or Bennie did every year when I was growing up. Now it's my turn to buy Isabel a cake so everyone on Gold Street can celebrate her birthday."

"And if you kids are lucky," said Grandma, "maybe one day it will be your turn to buy a cake to celebrate Isabel's birthday. Won't that be something?"

Momma and Bennie and Grandma laughed.

"Yes," said Momma, and she looked right at me.

**"Make new friends but keep the old,
One is silver and the other's gold."**

Entonces mi mami sacó su álbum de recuerdos.

—Miren, niños —dijo—. ¿Saben cómo sabía Isabel que habría pastel? —Mami señaló con el dedo una foto de Isabel soplando la vela de un pastel de cumpleaños.

Todos rodeamos a mi mami.

—¿Ven esta foto? —preguntó—. Es de la casa de al lado, la casa de tu abuelita, donde me crié.

—¡Y yo estoy ahí! —dije, señalando a una niña sentada junto a Isabel.

—No —dijo mami—. ¡Soy yo! Yo tenía la misma edad que tú ahora, y tu abuelita compró un pastel a Isabel, así como hacía ella o Bennie cada año durante mi niñez. Ahora me toca a mí comprarle un pastel a Isabel para que todos los de la calle Oro podamos festejar su cumpleaños.

—Y niños, si tienen suerte —dijo mi abuelita—, quizá algún día les toque a ustedes comprar un pastel para festejarle el cumpleaños a Isabel. ¿Se imaginan?

Mami y Bennie y abuelita se rieron.

—Sí —dijo mami, y me miró fijamente.

**—Los amigos que tienes son un tesoro
Los nuevos de plata, los viejos de oro.—**

Isabel, 2003

The Treasure on Gold Street is a story about a real person named Isabel. Isabel is an important part of our bilingual and bicultural neighborhood in central El Paso, a city located in West Texas on the U.S./Mexico border. The other characters in Isabel's story—Isabel's mother Benita, my granddaughter Hannah, her brother Johnny and the friend Erica she so admires across the street—are real, too.

Gold Street, though, is not really the name of our street. Gold Street is about five blocks south of Louisville Street where we have lived for the last 25 years. I borrowed that shimmering name—Gold Street—so I could talk about life's riches. I count Isabel as one of them.

Isabel was born on June 1, 1959. Because of an early illness, her brain may not have developed completely. This is called mental retardation.

People with mental retardation are limited in some ways. They may have some difficulty with skills that many of us take for granted, like learning to read or write, or doing math or talking clearly. They might have trouble making decisions or getting dressed, or eating or washing by themselves. They often act much younger than they really are.

People with mental retardation, though—just like people everywhere—often have certain strengths. And Isabel is no exception.

For instance, Isabel is most especially gifted when it comes to understanding vibrations and currents of feeling—things racing through the neighborhood that most of us ignore or are too busy to care about. To these, Isabel responds deeply. When something is not right with her mother Bennie, she gets very sad. On the other hand, she really gets excited and happy when her mother is happy, or when there is a party on the block, or a new baby, or someone comes to visit her mother or any of us neighbors. She'll arrive on your porch almost at the same time your visitors do.

In fact, when our family moved to this neighborhood, Isabel was the first person to greet us as we carried our suitcases and furniture through the front door.

Our daughter Susie was six years old at the time, our sons Johnny three and Andy two. They liked Isabel right away. She was big like an adult, but she didn't have any of those characteristics adults have that are so difficult: she didn't tell them what to do, she didn't boss them around, she didn't suddenly stand up and say she was leaving. She could come over early and stay all day. If my kids wanted to watch TV,

Isabel would sit and watch TV with them. She would laugh at all their jokes, even the ones that weren't funny. If they wanted to be pushed down the street on their tricycles all afternoon, she would do it. And she was strong enough to give a good push, and strong enough to catch them if they started to keel over.

But inevitably, when our kids—or any of the kids in the neighborhood—reached the age of five or six or seven, they began to look for kids their own age to play with; and somehow in that looking, they would realize that Isabel was big, really big—much too big—and they would be more interested in their peers and not in Isabel. This was hard for Isabel, you could see, but the hurt was softened somewhat by the fact that there was always a new little kid in the neighborhood who was ready to fall in love with her.

My daughter Susie grew up. She got married and she and her husband Eddie decided to buy the house next door to us, where they live with our grandkids, Hannah and Johnny Andrew. When Hannah turned three, Isabel came to visit. And Hannah and Isabel became inseparable, just the way Isabel had been with Susie.

We couldn't have asked for a better friend for our kids and grandkids.

— *Lee Byrd*

Drawing by Isabel

I wrote this book so that all the kids who have known and loved Isabel

will—when they get very old and very wise—remember what a treasure she is: a treasure and a really good friend.

For Isabel and Bennie and their family
For Susie, Eddie, John, Andy and Sandie
For Hannah, Johnny Andrew and Baby Ed, Santiago and Emma Birdie
For all the kids—old and young—in our neighborhood
&, most especially, for Bob.

Lee Merrill Byrd

Me gustaria poder detener un momento de la vida.

Para mi esposa Guadalupe.

Antonio Castro L.

For my wife Monica and my daughter Melina.

Antonio Castro H.

Treasure on Gold Street / El tesoro en la calle oro. Copyright © 2003 by Lee Merrill Byrd. Illustrations copyright © 2003 by Antonio Castro L. Translation by Sharon Franco copyright © 2003 by Cinco Puntos Press.

Grateful acknowledgement is made to Isela Gonzalez for permission to use her mother Benita and sister Isabel's names and images; to Tommy and Gracie Chavez for permission to use
their daughter Erica's name and image; to Edward Holland and Susannah Byrd for permission to use their children Hannah and John Andrew's names and images. Thanks to Hannah Hollandbyrd for her great background illustrations.

First Edition 10 9 8 7 6 5 4 3 2 1

Library of Congress Cataloging-in-Publication Data
Byrd, Lee Merrill. Treasure on Gold Street = El tesoro de la Calle Oro / by Lee Merrill Byrd ; illustrated by Antonio Castro L.—1st ed.
p. cm. Summary: Hannah describes her neighbors on Gold Street, especially Isabel, who is an adult but who still plays with the young children and holds her mother's hand to cross the street, just as she has since Hannah's mother was small.
ISBN-13 978-1-933693-11-8; ISBN-10: 1-933693-11-8 [1. People with mental disabilities—Fiction. 2. Neighbors—Fiction. 3. Neighborhood—Fiction. 4. Friendship—Fiction. 5. Spanish language materials—Bilingual.] I. Title: El tesoro de la Calle Oro. II.
Castro, Antonio,
1941- ill. III. Title. PZ73.B97 2003 [E]—dc21

2003003533

Collaborative illustration, book and cover design by Antonio Castro H.
Hats off to the dos Antonios!

More Bilingual Books for Kids from Cinco Puntos Press

The Day It Snowed Tortillas / El día que nevó tortillas, by Joe Hayes, illustrated by Antonio Castro L.

Pájaro verde / The Green Bird, by Joe Hayes, illustrated by Antonio Castro L.

¡Sí, se puede! / Yes, We Can, by Diana Cohn, illustrated by Francisco Delgado

Cada niño / Every Child, A Bilingual Songbook for Kids, by Tish Hinojosa, illustrated by Lucia Angela Perez

The Festival of Bones / El festival de las calaveras, A Little Bitty Book for the Day of the Dead, written and illustrated by Luis San Vicente

La Llorona, The Weeping Woman, by Joe Hayes, illustrated by Vicki Trego Hill

¡El Cucuy!, A Bogeyman Cuento in English & Spanish, by Joe Hayes, illustrated by Honorio Robledo

Little Gold Star / Estrellita de oro, A Cinderella Cuento, by Joe Hayes, illustrated by Gloria Osuna Perez and Lucia Angela Perez

Tell Me a Cuento / Cuéntame un story, by Joe Hayes, illustrated by Geronimo Garcia

Watch Out for Clever Women! / ¡Cuidado con las mujeres astutas!, by Joc Hayes, illustrated by Vicki Trego Hill

The Story of Colors / La historia de los colores, A Folktale from the Jungles of Chiapas, by Subcomandante Marcos, illustrated by Domitila Domínguez

A Gift from Papá Diego / Un regalo de Papá Diego, by Benjamin Alire Sáenz, illustrated by Geronimo Garcia

Grandma Fina and Her Wonderful Umbrellas / La Abuelita Fina y sus sombrillas maravillosas, by Benjamin Alire Sáenz, illustrated by Geronimo Garcia

Lover Boy / Juanito el Cariñoso, A Bilingual Counting Book by Lee Merrill Byrd, illustrated by Francisco Delgado

The King of Things / El rey de las cosas, written and illustrated by Artemio Rodríguez

CINCO PUNTOS PRESS
www.cincopuntos.com